ARTURO'S BATON

Written and Illustrated by Syd Hoff

Clarion Books/New York

Clarion Books
a Houghton Mifflin Company imprint
215 Park Avenue South, New York, NY 10003
Copyright © 1995 by Syd Hoff

The illustrations were executed in ink, watercolor dyes, and colored pencil.
The text was set in 16-point Times.

www.houghtonmifflinbooks.com

Printed in China

Library of Congress Cataloging-in-Publication Data

Hoff, Syd, 1912—
Arturo's baton / story and pictures by Syd Hoff.
p. cm.
Summary: When an orchestra conductor misplaces his baton and feels
he cannot work without it, he learns that it is his own talent, not a little
stick, that makes him famous.
ISBN 0-395-71020-0 PA ISBN 0-618-19597-1
[1. Conducting—Fiction.] I. Title.
PZ7.H672Ar   1996
[Fic]—dc20   94-34655
CIP   AC

SCP 10 9 8 7 6 5

For my father, who was a conductor,
but only on a streetcar

Arturo was a famous conductor.

When he waved his baton, the orchestra played.

He waved it wildly, and the trumpets blared.
He waved it gently, and the violins sighed.

"More! More!" shouted the people in the audience.

After the concert they swarmed around Arturo
just to be near him.
They brought him flowers.

"I thank you," said Arturo.
"This little stick, my baton, thanks you.
Without it I could never conduct."

Felix, his manager, drove Arturo home.
"Remember," Felix told Arturo,
"After tomorrow's concert,
you leave on a world tour."

The maid met Arturo with a tall glass of milk.
His dog, Toscanini, brought him his slippers.
The valet had his pajamas ready.

Arturo got into bed.
He put his baton on the pillow next to him.

In the morning the baton was gone!

The servants looked for it.
Felix looked for it,
Toscanini looked for it.
Even Arturo was down on his hands and knees, looking.

Finally they gave up.
"Cancel the concert! Cancel the tour!"
Arturo shouted.

"We can't cancel," said Felix.
"All the tickets are sold.
You'll just have to use another baton."

Felix drove Arturo to a big music store.

Arturo tried every baton they had.
"This one is too heavy," he said.
"This one is too light."

"This one's too long.
This one's too short.
It's no use,
I can't conduct without my baton!"

"You're a great conductor, Arturo," said Felix.
"You don't need a baton to make the orchestra play.
Just wave your hands."
"That won't work," said Arturo.
"But I will give it a try."

They hurried to the concert hall.

Arturo went onstage.
"Good luck!" said Felix.

Arturo stood in front of the orchestra
and waved his hands.

He waved them wildly, and the trumpets blared.
He waved them gently, and the violins sighed.

"More! More! Encore! Encore!"
shouted the people in the audience.

They rushed to the stage
and threw flowers at Arturo's feet.

"Bravo, maestro," said Felix.
"The orchestra never sounded better."
"You were right," Arturo whispered to Felix.
"I *am* a great conductor."

Arturo's maid and valet were waiting for him
in his dressing room.
"Look what someone found!" the maid said.

There stood Toscanini
with Arturo's baton in his mouth!

"Thanks, Toscanini," said Arturo,
"but I will not be needing it anymore.
It's yours to keep."

And they flew off on the world tour.